Margaret
Mahy

The Midnight Story

`D1136842`

PENGUIN BOOKS

PENGUIN BOOKS

Published by the Penguin Group
Penguin Books Ltd, 27 Wrights Lane, London w8 5tz, England
Penguin Books USA Inc., 375 Hudson Street, New York, New York 10014, USA
Penguin Books Australia Ltd, Ringwood, Victoria, Australia
Penguin Books Canada Ltd, 10 Alcorn Avenue, Toronto, Ontario, Canada m4v 3b2
Penguin Books (NZ) Ltd, 182–190 Wairau Road, Auckland 10, New Zealand

Penguin Books Ltd, Registered Offices: Harmondsworth, Middlesex, England

First published in *The Chewing-Gum Rescue* by J. M. Dent & Sons Ltd 1982
Published in Puffin Books 1992

This collection published in Penguin Books 1996
3 5 7 9 10 8 6 4 2

Copyright © Margaret Mahy, 1982
All rights reserved

Set in 12.5/14.5pt Bembo Monotype
Typeset by Datix International Limited, Bungay, Suffolk
Printed in England by Clays Ltd, St Ives plc

Contents

The Chewing-Gum Rescue

ON the evening of pocket-money day Mr Frisbee came stumping along to his own back door after shutting up his prize-winning angora goats, Gregorius and Gertrude, for the night. He had been very careful about this for the infamous Gargle Goat Thief Gang was roaming around the countryside, stealing goats of all kinds – very worrying for goat owners. Mr Frisbee was looking forward to a quiet evening with his wife and children. But as he was wiping his weary feet in their faithful gumboots, suddenly the gumboots stuck to the doormat and he fell head-over-heels into the hall.

'Help! Help!' shouted Mr Frisbee as he lay there, his feet up in the air and the doormat still stuck to his boots. His five daughters, Florence, Flora, Fenella, Felicity and the baby Francesca, came running to see what had happened to their loving father.

'Oh Dad!' cried Florence. 'You have trodden on a piece of Francesca's chewing-gum.'

'Yes,' said Flora. 'You know, Dad! It's on the telly.'

'It's on the doormat too,' grumbled Mr Frisbee shaking his feet out of their faithful gumboots.

'It's advertised on television,' Flora explained. 'It's Dr Gumption's simply Great Green Gum with the Dairy Fresh Mint Flavour.'

'It's full of fluoride and chlorophyll and it's the gum that's good for the gums,' said Felicity.

'And it's got champion chewability,' finished Fenella as she helped Felicity pull the doormat away from the gumboots. It took a lot of doing.

'Can't you have ice-cream instead?' asked Mr Frisbee fretfully.

And Florence, Flora, Felicity, Fenella and even Francesca replied as one daughter, 'Mum won't let us.'

'Of course I won't,' said Mrs Frisbee firmly, for she was a dentist during the day, and disapproved of sweets and cakes which, as everyone knows, are so bad for children's teeth. 'No ice-creams in this house, no chocolate or sherbert or coconut cream caramels or butterscotch! No fudge or toffee-apples, no brown sugar peanut brittle, and no buttery molasses taffy. Dr Gumption's Gum is the only thing I'm prepared to tolerate. I want all my daughters to have teeth as strong as tigers' teeth and as beautiful as pearls.'

Well, that very night, after the girls had eaten all their greens, chewed their crusts twenty-five times each and had each finished off with a raw carrot, they sat down to watch television. But no sooner had the television set been switched on than Dr Gumption himself appeared, smiling and scraping all over the screen.

'Hey kids!' he cried. 'It's good GOOD news. Dr Gumption has a great new gum on the market and – wow – it's twice as sticky and – mmmmmmmmmm – it's twice as stretchy and – YAY – it's twice as green and it's got double that super duper minty flavour, so listen kids, to what everyone is saying . . .'

And then a chorus of beautiful girls in green clustered around Dr Gumption and they sang . . .

'Do friends avoid you? Take the hint!
Chew Dr Gumption's Minty-mint.'

'Shall we?' Florence signalled to her sisters by wiggling her crooked eyebrows.

'Next pocket-money day!' Flora signalled back with hers.

Next pocket-money day Mr Frisbee came home after locking up his prize angora goats with tremendous care and he found that the back door wouldn't even open; he had to go round to the front door like a polite visitor. As he came in the smell of minty-mint rolled towards him like a great green ocean.

'What's happened to the back door?' he demanded crossly.

'It's got a piece of Felicity's gum stuck in

it,' said Flora, telling tales as she often did.

'Fenella made me put it there,' grumbled Felicity. 'She said . . . "Just for fun put your gum here!" and when I did, she shut the door on it and now we can't get the door open, and my gum has gone for good.'

'Honestly, my dear,' Mr Frisbee said to his wife, 'a simple orange each would save a lot of trouble in the long run.'

'Never!' declared Mrs Frisbee (Dentist). 'I spend all day patching up teeth ruined by coco-nut candy and frosted cakes. Never shall my daughters feast on brandy balls or barley sugar, Turkish delight, marshmallows or chocolate pea-nuts. They shall have teeth as strong as tigers' teeth and as beautiful as pearls.'

But later, when the lid of the piano refused to open because Francesca's gum was jammed under it, Mrs Frisbee looked very thoughtful and still later, when the tablecloth stuck to the table just as if it had been nailed at all four corners, she looked quite cross. 5

That very night on television the beaming face of Dr Gumption appeared once more.

'Hey kids, hey!' he shouted. 'Boy oh boy! What news! Dr Gumption's Gum has been improved yet again. Triple Chewability! Quadruple stretch power. Ten times the stickability! Oh that gloptious Gumption Gum. It's the NOW gum! It's the POW gum! And don't forget, kids, it's got that triple ripple super duper minty-mint flavour.' And the girls in green appeared and sang . . .

'Make your father go all numb!
Chew Dr Gumption's Gloptious Gum!'

'Shall we?' signalled Florence with her crooked eyebrows.

'Yes, yes yes!' signalled Flora, Felicity, Fenella and Francesca.

A week later on pocket-money day Mr Frisbee came home having shut his precious Gregorius and Gertrude away for the night.

6 'The Gargle Gang will never get them,' he

muttered fiercely to himself. 'But locking up is hard work. I'm longing for a cup of tea.' He stumped up the path in his faithful gumboots but he could not open the back door or the front door either. Most of the windows were sealed shut, too, but at last he found that he could open the bathroom window with a stick, and by standing on an up-ended apple box he was able to somersault into his house.

Inside, the smell of Super Duper Minty-mint was so strong he staggered back clutching his throat. Dr Gumption's chewing-gum stretched everywhere in an evil green web. It was as if a whole houseful of wicked spiders had been at work for a week. It seized your shoes and stuck them to the floor, it caught your coat and held on to your hair. It was like a super duper minty-mint mad monster from Mars stretching from room to room to room to room.

'Arrrrrh!' cried Mr Frisbee, as his five daughters and Mrs Frisbee came to meet him, climbing nimbly through the sticky maze. 7

'Couldn't you let them have a liquorice all-sort each instead?' he gasped.

'No, no!' replied Mrs Frisbee. 'I'm a dentist as well as a mother. If you saw the horrors that I see every day – molars molested and melted away by refined sugars – you would understand. Never shall my little ones have peppermint creams or coconut ice, boiled lollies, dolly mixtures, raspberry drops, oddfellows, humbugs, jujubes or all-day suckers. My daughters must have teeth as strong as tigers' teeth and as beautiful as pearls.'

'I suppose they must,' said Mr Frisbee wearily.

At dinner that night the soup tasted of Dr Gumption's Super Duper Minty-mint Gum. The roast beef, roast potatoes, roast onions, roast parsnips, roast pumpkin and buttered beans all tasted of Dr Gumption's Super Duper Minty-mint Gum and so did the wholesome apple-brown-betty and the raw carrots to finish off with. No one enjoyed anything very much.

Yet that very night on television Dr

Gumption appeared again. 'Hey kids!' he shouted. 'Hey – all you gum chewers out there! Have you tried Dr Gumption's NEW splendiferous magniferous gum? Such expansion. Such extension! It stretches up and out and every whichever way. It's the fun gum that keeps the household happy and healthy. It sticks so well that it's being used by boat builders as a saltwater glue. And it's got that unutterable, that entirely inexpressible super duper triple ripple more-minty-than-mint flavour. WOW!'

Then the girls in green appeared and sang . . .

'Want to make your teacher squint?
Chew Dr Gumption's Minty-mint.'

'Next time!' Florence signalled Flora, Felicity, Fenella and Francesca, wiggling her eyebrows in time to the music.

A week later on pocket-money day Mr Frisbee staggered up to bed coughing and choking and fighting off green tentacles of gum.

'Man can triumph over any odds,' he muttered. 'He can get used to anything if he has to.' He was a bit lonely because Mrs Frisbee was out at a Dental Health Conference.

What Mr Frisbee did not know was that Florence, Flora, Felicity, Fenella and even Francesca all had packets of Dr Gumption's New More-minty-than-mint Gum tucked under their pillows. They hadn't started chewing it yet because they had some of the old Triple Minty-mint Gum from last week's pocket-money day to use up first.

As he lay awake, missing Mrs Frisbee B.D.S., Mr Frisbee heard strange shufflings and muffled bleats coming from the goat pens. They were not very loud and, had Mrs Frisbee been at home, he would have been sound asleep and would have missed hearing them altogether. As it was he leaped to his feet and peeped out of the window. What a sight met his eyes!

There were the five dreadful Gargle brothers, leaders of the Gargle Goat Thief Gang, not to mention five of their minions. They were in the actual act of stealing Gregorius and Gertrude, Mr Frisbee's prize-winning angoras. There was not a moment to be lost.

Wrapping his hands in Mrs Frisbee's second-best petticoat and seizing a strand of Dr Gumption's Triple Super Duper Minty-mint Gum that happened to be dangling from the guttering, Mr Frisbee swung down like Tarzan, a curiously splendid figure in his simulated leopardskin pyjamas, screaming reprimands and reproaches at the villainous goat thieves.

Florence and Flora woke up at once and looked out of the window. What they saw horrified them and they hastened to wake up Felicity, Fenella and even Francesca by way of reinforcements. Armed only with Dr Gumption's New More-minty-than-mint Gum, they climbed out of the bathroom window and whisked over to the goat pens.

For there was no doubt that Mr Frisbee was getting the worst of it.

In his first spectacular swing he had struck Harvey Gargle to the ground and then as he swept majestically back he had struck Ellis Gargle, knocking out his false teeth and seriously bewildering him. But then he himself hit the side of the house very hard and let go the chewing-gum, falling dazed to the ground, an easy prey to the infuriated goat thieves.

Mad Rory Gargle with two minions advanced upon him in a threatening way; Bernard Gargle (with two other minions) picked up his fallen brothers, not forgetting Ellis's false teeth, while Rackham Gargle with the single remaining minion rapidly led Gregorious Goat and his nanny wife, Gertrude, towards a waiting van.

Victory was within the grasp of the nefarious goat thieves. All seemed lost . . .

When, suddenly, with a lion-like roar Florence sprang out at them from the right, biting firmly into a piece of Dr Gumption's New More-minty-than-mint Gum as she did so.

Flora bounded in from the left, whooping and hooting like a whole treeful of owls. There was a hearty hullabaloo from Fenella who, chewing her piece of Dr Gumption's New More-minty-than-mint Gum, came up behind Florence, a blood-curdling growl from Felicity leaping out of the chrysanthemums, and squeaks and squeals from Francesca who rose up out of the watering-can.

The goat thieves were entirely taken aback. This unexpected racket and rumpus-bumpus upset them badly.

'Squad ... breathe OUT!' shouted Florence and the daughters of the house breathed out as one combined daughter. A terrible wave of un-utterable, indescribable, inexpressible, super duper triple ripple more-minty-than-mint aroma swept over the goat thieves.

'Enemy Mint Gas Attack!' shouted Mad Rory Gargle before he dropped like a stone. Ellis and Rackham Gargle and the assorted minions keeled over like slender reeds in a 13 hurricane and even the goats fell to their knees gasping.

Mr Frisbee, however, had been exposed to Dr Gumption's punishing mint flavour for at least three weeks and although somewhat unsteady, he was not totally overcome. He had built up an immunity.

'Tie them up!' he ordered. 'Quickly.'

His devoted daughters did not hesitate. Within a moment the Gargle Gang were wound around with Dr Gumption's powerful product. The music died down and the goats began to revive. At this very moment Mrs Frisbee drove the family car into the yard. She was astonished to find it filled with disabled goat thieves, groggy goats, her husband bruised but resplendent in his simulated leopardskin pyjamas, not to mention her five daughters still up well beyond their bedtime.

'You see how wise I was,' she said. 'You couldn't have saved Gregorius and Gertrude
14 with a piece of Turkish delight.'

'I'll never say anything against Dr Gumption's Mintier-than-mint Gum again,' Mr Frisbee vowed fervently.

Florence looked at her sisters. 'Shall I tell him?' she signalled with her crooked eyebrows.

'O.K.,' they all signalled back.

'Actually, Dad,' said Florence, 'we're getting rather sick of it.'

'Well, that's all right, my dear,' said Mrs Frisbee quickly, 'because I heard of a delicious new sweet at the Conference today. Honey Bliss it's called and it's made with pure golden honey collected from lime blossoms by particularly happy and busy bees. Of course you'll still have to brush your teeth after it, but you have to do that anyway.'

Florence, Flora, Felicity, Fenella and Francesca looked delighted to hear this. They had enjoyed Dr Gumption's Gum but it was very hard work keeping it under control and they needed a rest.

The police came and took the goat thieves away. 'We've been waiting a long time to get our hands on this lot,' the Chief Constable said. 'There's a big reward, you know. You'll be able to extend your herd of angora goats.'

Mr Frisbee, though bruised and battered, beamed with joy.

Shortly after this Dr Gumption's Gum was withdrawn from the market and only used again in army exercises. Florence, Flora, Felicity, Fenella and Francesca settled down with Honey Bliss which smelt deliciously of lime blossom and tasted wonderful. However, it must be noted that when Gertrude the goat had two beautiful kids a short time later they did have, very faintly, a mintier-than-mint perfume, no doubt due to their mother's exposure to Dr Gumption's Gum during the great mintier-than-mint goat rescue and the heroic victory of the Frisbee sisters, all of whom grew up to have teeth as strong as tigers' teeth and as beautiful as pearls.

The Midnight Story on Griffon Hill

MARTIN and Micky Ingoldsby loved swimming. They could do back stroke, breast stroke, and butterfly. They could do dog paddle, duck paddle and Australian crawl. All who saw them in the school swimming pool were heard to remark, 'Those boys are natural swimmers.'

'Yes,' their sports teacher would say, 'and it's really amazing because they spend most of their time looking after their father, and don't get a chance to do much swimming at all – just a little bit during the lunch hour at school.'

Martin and Micky dreamed of water and swimming, of green rivers and blue oceans, of glassy pools and sparkling lakes. However, they seldom managed to visit the seaside or the river-side or the lakeside because their father was always too busy to take them.

They lived with their industrious parent in a 17

tall house surrounded by a tangly garden at the foot of Griffon Hill – one of those alarming bony hills with wild paths leading nowhere, fierce rocks, and the feeling of having an ancient secret held in its dark heart. Griffons had once lived in the caves and caverns of Griffon Hill and sometimes it seemed that the air still throbbed with the beat of their great eaglish wings and echoed with their lionish cries. If you were lucky you might find a fossilized griffon feather or griffon's paw-mark, and at the back gate of the Ingoldsby house was a big stony pit where men had once dug for the griffon's treasure, without ever finding it. It was said that the last of the griffons had wept a fortune in pearls, but if it was true there was no proof of it. The pearls had gone for ever. Although it was strange and lonely, Martin and Micky loved living by mysterious Griffon Hill in the heart of a tangly garden, but they did wish there was some place close at hand where they could practise their swimming, They liked the thought of being champions.

Mr Ingoldsby, their father, was a famous author and his speciality was fun. On Monday he wrote spritely stories and farcical fiction for a family magazine. On Tuesday he would type a laughable legend for the local radio. On Wednesday he would dash off a merry memoir for the *Weekly Wonder*, while on Thursday he wrote some humorous history for the *Evening Egghead*, and on Friday he'd concoct a comical chronicle for the *Householders', Ratepayers' and Pennypinchers' Advertiser*.

His stories were so funny that doctors gave them to people suffering from dejections, doldrums or despondency or even to those who were merely down in the dumps. As the patients read his stories they would begin to simper and smile; they would grin and giggle and guffaw, and at last they would laugh loud and long until they were light-hearted again. Then, when they left the doctor's surgery, they would run straight off to the library to borrow more of these marvellous stories collected in books – they kept melancholy at bay so very successfully.

The trouble was that being funny the whole time, though very good for other people, was very bad for Mr Ingoldsby. It put him all out of balance. There were times when he longed to write a quiet story or even a sad one. Sometimes it seemed to him that underneath all the chuckling and chortling in his books he could hear the sound of someone weeping, silently and secretly, a mysterious weeping that no one else seemed to notice. Being perpetually humorous made him very bad-tempered, and the funnier he was in his books the crosser he was at home. It wasn't much fun for Martin and Micky living with such a crabby father. Of course they could read his books to remind themselves how nice he could be, but it wasn't as good as if he'd been cheerful with them in the first place.

Every weekend Mr Ingoldsby was busy with typing, checking, putting in the full-stops that had tried to escape and so on. It wasn't work he enjoyed, and one particular weekend he had 20 only just begun to do it, and was already having trouble with an unruly comma, when there came a knock on his door.

'Go away!' he shouted. However, the knocking came again, quiet but very determined. Mr Ingoldsby threw a slipper at the door in a fretful way, but the door took no notice and actually opened a little bit. Martin looked cautiously in, just above the door-handle, and Micky looked nervously in just below it.

'What do you want?' cried Mr Ingoldsby. 'You know I'm busy.'

'Dad, we've made the beds and we've vacuumed the house,' Martin said.

'So what!' shouted his irascible parent.

'We've swept the cobwebs and frightened the spiders,' squeaked Micky.

'Big deal!' growled Mr Ingoldsby, still thinking of that wretched comma.

'We've done the dishes and wiped the bench and hung out the washing, and ironed the handkerchiefs and polished the sideboard, the silver and the shoes,' said Martin, 'and now we'd love 21 to go swimming. Summer's almost over and soon it will be too cold for us to enjoy swimming until next spring.'

'Please take us!' Micky begged. 'Last year I could swim like a fish but now I'm almost back to a mere dog paddle. I'm forgetting how to dive. I'm almost forgetting how to get wet. Please, Dad!'

'You want *me* to take you . . . *me*, with all my work!' exclaimed Mr Ingoldsby. 'Look at it . . . Friday's comical chronicle and Tuesday's laughable legend still full of spelling mistakes, and commas thinking they can do anything they like. I'm up to HERE with work,' cried Mr Ingoldsby holding his hand well over his head and working himself into an enjoyable fury, 'and if I don't get it done, well, you know what! Bills mounting up. Empty money-boxes, bank balance collapsing. Calamity! Catastrophe! – And that's not counting the poor suffering mortals in the outside world who won't have anything to laugh 22 at! There'll be outbreaks of glumness, I tell you, epidemics of depression. The country will sink beneath waves of gloom, and you'll be the ones to blame, with your selfish demands for swimming and salt water. It's just as well someone's got some sense of responsibility around here. Now get out and leave me to work.'

Martin sighed, but Micky couldn't help shouting back, 'We cook your dinner and clean your shoes but you don't take us anywhere. You're mean. You're only nice in books, never ever in real life.'

Martin pulled Micky away, just before Mr Ingoldsby threw his second slipper at them, hitting the wall exactly where Micky's nose had been only a moment before. They ran off, disappointed and disconsolate, and Mr Ingoldsby, after a bit of snarling, returned to his comical chronicle. But somehow or other he had lost interest in that tricky comma. He left it sitting in the wrong place and sat back pondering gloomily.

'I should have taken the boys swimming,' he thought, 'I'm a terrible father. If only I could tell them how sick of it I am . . . all this ha! ha! ha! and ho! ho! ho! If only they knew that I'm saving to build a little swimming pool in our own back garden as a splendid surprise. But if I told them it wouldn't be a surprise any more. And I'm not even sure I'm going to be able to afford it anyway – not unless I finish these two humorous histories. Oh, it's more than I can bear!'

And he snatched up his pen and began work at once on an entirely new story, a sad story, a story like a lonely song sung on a day of grey slanting rain and falling leaves. There wasn't a laugh in it from beginning to end for it told of the death of the griffons and the downfall of the good giants. It told of the wizards growing old and forgetting their spells of kindness, wandering off down the rough roads of the world on bruised and bleeding feet, of flying horses shot down with arrows, of griffons' eggs growing cold in forgotten caves and little griffons dying in their chilly shells. No one came any longer to rescue the princesses. They died too, alone in ancient towers, and birds made nests out of their shining hair.

As he wrote, tears like commas of glass ran down Mr Ingoldsby's nose and plopped on to his paper, which was soon punctuated with blisters of wetness.

Late in the afternoon, when he had finished his first and only melancholy tale, he blotted his eyes and his nose and spoke sternly to himself.

'Who would want to read this? There's enough sadness in the world already. Don't get carried away by melancholy, Allardyce Ingoldsby.' So saying he opened his window and looked out on the steep, secret slopes of Griffon Hill where the wind was turning cart-wheels all the way from its rocky crest down into the tangles of Mr Ingoldsby's own garden, spinning like a cog in the year's machinery which was pushing the world on towards autumn, winter and then spring again. The wind built it-self towers of late-summer leaves, a whole rustling 25 city of castles, which it let fall away through its careless hands. It turned the trees into harps and ran its fingers through the green hair of the grass. Mr Ingoldsby watched it and, smiling sadly, posted the pages of his story one by one out of the window.

'No one would have wanted to read it anyway,' he mumbled, watching the wind trundle it, page by page, over the ground and then whirl it like a flight of crumpled birds high against the dark cone of Griffon Hill.

Mr Ingoldsby padded out to the kitchen. 'I'm sorry I was so cross,' he said to his sons. 'I didn't mean to be like that. We'll go swimming now if you like.'

'It's late,' Martin said. 'Too late . . . look at the long shadows.'

'Look at the clock!' said Micky. 'It's potato-peeling, carrot-scraping time.'

'First thing tomorrow!' Mr Ingoldsby promised. 'We'll go absolutely first thing tomorrow. Let's get up really early.'

Late that night just as Mr Ingoldsby was getting into bed something tapped at his window. At first he thought a long white face was looking in at him, but then he saw it was a page of typing paper plastered flat against the glass.

'I weep for the death of griffons, those noble beasts of the world's morning,' he read. It was the first page of his story. It clung there for a moment, and then the night took it back again. It was like a lonely white moth fluttering away.

'What sort of father am I?' wondered Mr Ingoldsby, feeling sorry for his poor crumpled story. 'I'm not very nice to my boys, and I throw my sad stories away because they don't match the funny ones that went before. And after all *I* liked it, even if no one else did. Perhaps I'll just go and see if it's still blowing around in the garden, and take another look at it.'

He put on his tartan dressing-gown, took Micky's butterfly net and set off into the warm and windy night, under a sky as clear as deep blue glass, all shiny with the light of a full moon.

Mr Ingoldsby thought he saw the page of his story flapping ahead of him, like a ghost with corners. He lifted the skirts of his tartan dressing-gown with one hand and waved the butterfly net with the other as he set off through the garden, past the pit where no one had found any treasure, and along the zig-zag path that led up Griffon Hill. Up and up he went, huffing and puffing like a little tartan steam engine, this way and that, swooping and scooping with the butterfly net, almost but never quite catching his sad, flyaway story. The path ended, but Mr Ingoldsby could hear the vast soft voice of the late summer night whispering, 'I weep for the death of the griffons, those noble beasts of the world's morning.' Path or no path he went on, leaping and scooping but never quite catching his runaway pages though his story was being whispered in the very air around him.

Suddenly something moved above him and the moon seemed to go behind a cloud. Mr Ingoldsby had run between two great paws, like the paws of a lion but much bigger. He looked up and then up still further. What seemed just another one of the strangely shaped rocks of Griffon Hill was a huge creature, part eagle, part lion, sitting back on its hindlegs, slowly folding its wings behind it and turning its head down to look at him. It had a hooked beak and wild dark eyes, each one reflecting a full moon so that it seemed to have pupils of silver fire. Mr Ingoldsby was standing between the paws of a fabulous beast . . . perhaps the original and ancient griffon that had given Griffon Hill its name. Its front legs were the claws of an eagle and in its right claw it held the flighty page of Mr Ingoldsby's story.

'So it's you that has been covering the hill with these tumbling pages,' it said. 'That's spreading litter, that is, and the punishment is a very tasty one.'

'Tasty?' quavered Mr Ingoldsby, overwhelmed by the size and the power of the fabulous Griffon.

'Tasty for me, that is,' the Griffon said. 'You'll have to be eaten. If we griffons catch anyone throwing wastepaper around on our hill we're allowed to eat them. It's a very old law and a lot of people have forgotten about it but it's in the books.'

'I didn't know,' Mr Ingoldsby said hastily.

'No excuse! Ignorance of the law is no excuse,' replied the griffon snapping its sharp beak – rather unpleasantly. 'You've been spreading wastepaper and must pay the penalty.'

'But it isn't really wastepaper,' Mr Ingoldsby cried. 'This is a story that I happened to lose earlier in the day. I was just trying to find it again. You could see that for yourself.'

The Griffon lifted its crest in sudden interest. 'A story?' it cried. 'A real old-fashioned sort of story? A tale? One I haven't heard before?'

'You won't have heard this one. It's just been written this afternoon,' said Mr Ingoldsby boldly. 'It wasn't there this morning.'

'I haven't heard a story in years, not a new

one, that is,' the Griffon said. 'Of course we've never ever given up telling the old ones. I do hope it's funny. I like a good laugh.'

Mr Ingoldsby sighed. 'Not very funny,' he had to confess. 'It's rather sad.'

'I'm not so fond of sad stories,' said the Griffon looking thoughtful. 'I'll tell you what . . . you read it and I'll see what I think of it. If I think it's rubbish after all I'll eat you, but if I happen to like it I'll let you go. Does that seem fair?'

'Not very,' Mr Ingoldsby replied.

'Well, let's put it like this . . .' said the Griffon. 'It's almost too fair from a griffon's point of view. I know some griffons who would make you read the story and then eat you anyway, no matter whether it was good or bad. Many griffons would think I was being unnaturally soft-hearted.'

'I don't have the rest of the story,' Mr Ingoldsby said, but the Griffon lifted its huge tail which was almost exactly like a lion's tail, except 31 that it ended in a point rather like the tip of a spear, and there, spiked neatly through each right-hand corner, were all the pages of Mr Ingoldsby's only sad story.

So there was nothing for it . . . he sat like a tartan gnome shuffling his pages and putting them into order while his companion looked over his shoulder with interested, moony eyes. Mr Ingoldsby did think of making a run for it but the Griffon, almost as if it was reading his thoughts, put its right front claws through the hem of his dressing-gown. There was nothing for it but to begin reading . . . reading by the moonlight caught and reflected and magnified by the Griffon's great eyes.

'I weep for the death of the griffons, those noble beasts of the world's morning.' He nearly choked with terror but the Griffon merely sighed and seemed to settle down to listen even more closely, so he went on. At first he read hesitating and stammering with fear, but the story – his only sad story – was stronger than his fear. He began to forget that he was a little fat man with a bad temper and a tartan dressing-gown who might be eaten at any moment, and he became simply a voice that the story was using to tell itself. In the small space between the Griffon's paws he stamped up and down waving his hands, while tears at his own words poured down his cheeks, and read his only sad story like a man singing a new song. Above him the Griffon listened in silence, and beyond the Griffon, the hill and the shiny night listened too. At last he came to the final page and the story ended, as it had begun, with tears for the passing of the griffons, the noble beasts of the world's morning.

Then Mr Ingoldsby grew quiet and the mysteriousness of Griffon Hill crept back around him. He remembered who he was and that he lost his temper too much, and that he had been telling a griffon story to a griffon on Griffon's Hill, prancing around like a piece of tumbling waste-paper himself.

'Go on, eat me,' he said, and wished he had taken his boys swimming every weekend, feeling sad for the time with them that he had missed. He looked up bravely at the fierce eagle face above him. Beside the moon reflected in each of its eyes he saw a star that swelled and changed and became a silver comet running shimmering down to the cruel beak. The Griffon was crying too.

Two enormous tears fell with a silvery splash at Mr Ingoldsby's feet and then rolled like great pearls down the hillside. Then two more tears fell and another two.

'How beautiful,' said the Griffon at last. 'How truly beautiful. How did you come to understand so much about griffons?'

'Perhaps it's living at the foot of Griffon Hill,' Mr Ingoldsby suggested. 'Perhaps I've picked some griffonish feeling out of the air.'

'Have you any more stories like that?' asked the fabulous creature eagerly.

'Well no . . . it's been very difficult . . .' Mr

Ingoldsby began, and before he knew what he was doing he was explaining all about his funny stories, and the sad stories that nobody would be interested in.

'I'm interested,' said the Griffon. 'I didn't think I would be but I am. And not only that, other griffons will be too. We're not really dead, as you can see. We've crept down into the heart of the world and only come out at full moon, just to check up on things. And griffons enjoy a good cry though it takes a lot to get them going. Mere sadness isn't enough. Griffons need power and poetry and a feeling of passing time. Now read your story all over again and I'll just sit here and drink it in. And then we'll see if we can't come to some arrangement – as between a griffon and a near neighbour.'

Mr Ingoldsby came staggering home in the early morning. The wind had died down and the sky was starting to be blue. The horizon, hung with flags of gold, was getting ready to welcome 35 the sun while over in the west, the moon was going down. Everything in the world seemed beautiful and perfectly in balance, even Mr Ingoldsby himself. He had read his story over and over again to the Griffon and though he did not read it as well as he had read it the first time, the Griffon had wept its great pearly tears at every repetition. Mr Ingoldsby had promised to write more sad stories and to come back to read them to the Griffon Hill griffons at the time of the next full moon. He felt very much at ease with the world as he came down the last slope to his back gate. Even the thought of frivolous fiction and merry memoirs did not worry him. In fact he found himself rather looking forward to writing them again. Someone was calling him. 'Dad! Dad!' He looked around, suddenly dazzled, for the thin bright rind of the sun pushed itself up above the horizon at that moment and reflected straight into his eyes. But what was it reflecting from? Martin and Micky, very dashing and cheerful in towels and swimming togs, came shouting out of the daze and dazzle.

'How did you manage it? It's brilliant,' they cried.

It *was* brilliant too. The stone pit where nobody had ever found any treasure was filled with wonderful warm salty water, clear as crystal but with moonlight and starlight caught in its depths. Mr Ingoldsby saw at once what had happened. The Griffon's tears had rolled down the hill and had filled the pit, turning it into a little warm lake deep enough for diving, just right for every kind of swimming. It was almost like having a midsummer seaside on your very doorstep. Martin and Micky knew their father had arranged it somehow but they couldn't work out just how, and their father didn't tell them. A man has to keep some secrets to himself.

And ever afterwards Mr Ingoldsby was as chirpy as a cricket – writing funny stories during the week, just as he always had. But at the weekends he wrote stories of beautiful sadness and 37 every full moon he climbed up Griffon Hill to read them, not only to his own Griffon but to the Griffon's beautiful griffon wife and aged griffon parents who listened, enraptured, to the melodious and melancholy tales. Sometimes, quite frequently really, they wept great tears that topped up the old treasure-pit with water that was warm but still sparkling so that Martin and Micky swam every day and their friends often came to swim too. Martin and Micky quickly became swimming champions at their school, darting through the water like moonbeams. For who could help being a very special swimmer if he practised in the tears of the fabulous griffons of Griffon Hill?

The Travelling Boy and the Stay-at-Home Bird

SAM lived with his anxious Great Aunt Angela in a house with high hedges and a closed gate. When she was behind her high hedge with the gate slammed shut Great Aunt Angela was happy. Jaunts, junkets and journeys worried her to bits, but a closed gate soothed her, smoothed her, made her feel serene. In her little sun-porch she would knit and sew and sing like a spring blackbird and, sometimes, snatch a catnap as well, whereas a journey, even to the shops, made her go all fidgety and fretful. At such times she became a very difficult Great Aunt for a boy like Sam.

Sam had eyes halfway between sky-blue and sea-green. You never saw a boy with such a look of distance about him. There were a thousand journeys locked up inside him waiting to get out.

'Go here! Go there! Walk! Run! Skate! Sail! Fly!' said the voices in his head. 'Get there somehow!' But Sam was not allowed to do any of these things. The gate was always shut, and he was forbidden to go into the dirty, dangerous world outside.

Sometimes, however, Great Aunt Angela, though rather short-sighted herself, saw Sam's blue-green look of distance and overheard the echo of the voices inside his head.

'I suppose he needs some lively company,' she thought. 'I'm not very fond of animals, but perhaps a good, clean pet of some kind . . .' and, very bravely, she put on her boots and her good going-out coat, took her shopping trundler and called Sam. Then they set out together to visit the Paramount Pet Shop, which was all of two corners away. They crossed the street when the traffic-lights told them to cross and Sam could see four roads, all going in different directions. One road led to the sea, another to the moun-

40 tains, one pointed to the South Pole and another

to the Equator. He was surrounded by possible journeys and all the roads seemed to be saying, 'Take me! Take me!'

Men had made a hole in the street and its black mouth hissed, 'Down here! Down here!' as Sam went by. He looked up and the sky was filled with travellers . . . a Piper Cherokee plane from the aero club, a couple of ducks in search of the river, and a whole crowd of sparrows, flying in every direction. 'Up and away! Up and away!' they cried, but only Sam could hear them.

Great Aunt Angela's own ears were too full of rattling footsteps, roaring cars, and raging trucks to hear the voices of possible journeys crying out to her.

When they got to the Paramount Pet Shop there were pets of all kinds to choose from – dogs, cats, guinea pigs, rabbits – but Great Aunt Angela did not want anything that would jump up, track in dirt on its paws, or have babies.

'What about a bird?' said the pet shop man, a very secret-looking man, unusual to find behind 41 a public place like a shop counter. 'Their cages are very easy to clean. Sam could learn to do that for himself, couldn't you, Sam?'

'I don't want anything that has to live in a cage,' Sam said. 'I don't like cages.'

When the pet shop man heard this he gave Sam a very careful glance, and Sam stared back, and saw at once that the pet shop man was full of journeys too, but that his journeys had all been taken. He wore them openly on his face, which was lined like a map with the tracery of a thousand explorations.

'Why, I think I have just the pet for you, Sam,' he said at last. 'It's out the back because it's rather large.'

'I can't afford much!' cried Great Aunt Angela, anxious immediately. 'And we don't have much room.'

'Oh they're very cheap, these particular pets,' the pet shop man assured her. 'They're very hard to place because you've got to wait until the right customer comes along.' Then he went out into the back of the shop and returned a moment later with a bird following him . . . a tall bird, rather like a patchwork tea-cosy on long yellow legs, quite tame and looking as if it would be no trouble at all around the house.

'It's very brightly coloured,' Great Aunt Angela said nervously, for bright colours were part of the danger of the world to her.

'Oh, that could change,' the pet shop man said. 'He'll grow to whatever colour you need him to be. And he'll fit into any space you happen to have in the house. Fitting into available space is this bird's speciality. And he'll grow to the exact size that suits you.'

Great Aunt Angela was delighted to hear this. 'I do like him,' she decided. 'I love his blue eyes. We'll take him shall we, Sam, and we'll call him Norton after my late cousin Norton. He's got a look in his eyes that reminds me of dear Norton very strongly. You'll like that, won't you, Sam?'

'Yes thank you, Great Aunt Angela,' Sam replied.

But in his mind Sam called the bird Fernando Eagle, the freest name he could think of, a name for some buccaneer or bold adventurer who also happened to be a bird.

'He's too tame, really,' Sam thought. 'He's *over*-tamed, but I'll un-tame him. I'll teach him to fight and fly and to be free, and when he does fly away at last — well, it will be almost as good as flying away myself. It will be a kind of promise to me that some day I'll be free too.'

Great Aunt Angela paid the money, and Sam and she walked home through the rattling, roaring, raging streets while Fernando Eagle stalked after them like a particularly well-behaved dog.

At home, with the gate closed and locked, Great Aunt Angela gave Sam and Fernando Eagle a slice of bread and jam each.

'He needs worms and wigglies, not bread and jam,' Sam cried.

'Oh Sam, don't say such things!' Great Aunt Angela exclaimed in alarm. 'I can't bear to think of worms and wigglies. And look —' she added triumphantly – 'he's eaten the bread and jam and he's asking for more.'

And so he had, and so he was.

'Good bird, Norton!' said Great Aunt Angela, patting him on the head.

Sam saw he had no time to lose and began his plans for the un-taming of Fernando Eagle immediately.

'He hasn't got a mother to teach him,' thought Sam, 'so I'll have to be a sort of mother to him.'

He tried to make himself as much like Fernando Eagle's mother as he could.

First he cut a bird mask out of cardboard but, when he tried it on, Fernando Eagle looked doubtful. Then he wrapped himself in an old curtain covered in red, white and blue squares, but Fernando Eagle merely sighed and shuffled his feet.

'Feet!' thought Sam and he cut himself big bird feet and stuck them on to the soles of his school shoes with sticky tape. Then he painted his new feet and his old legs (up above sock level) with yellow poster paint, and looked hopefully at Fernando Eagle. But Fernando Eagle sank his head deep into his ruff and clacked his beak in alarm.

'Now!' Sam cried. 'Listen! This is how eagles call,' and he hopped around the room giving wild dangerous cries of the sort he thought a free bird ought to give, as it took off into the sky. Such cries had never been heard behind the high hedge before. Out in the sun-porch Great Aunt Angela started as if she had been stung and dropped several stitches. Even so, she was not as frightened as Fernando Eagle who ran behind a chair and cowered there, terrified.

'Sam! Sam!' cried Great Aunt Angela as she burst into Sam's room. 'What a noise! Look at the room! Look at your legs! Look at those scraps of cardboard, look at your feet! Look at your face! Look at poor Norton, he's petrified, poor bird, and no wonder! Clean yourself up at once and then sweep the floor! Goodness gracious, what an example to set an innocent pet barely in the house thirty minutes. He'll think you're some sort of hoodlum or noodlum, Sam.'

She went out of the room and Fernando Eagle scuttled after her, anxious for quiet dignified company and more bread and jam. Sam was left to tidy up the mess he'd made. He was disappointed but not discouraged.

'It's a beginning,' he thought. 'I suppose it *is* pretty confusing for a bird before he realizes what he's supposed to do. But once he catches on he'll love it. Fancy being able to fly! I wish I could. I'll give him a flying-from-tree-to-tree lesson tomorrow and see how he gets on. I want him to be free as air . . . as free as – as a bird.'

In the middle of Great Aunt Angela's little square of lawn was a small tree, doing its best to be a tree in spite of being barbered and bobbed every spring and autumn. Still, if you really wanted to you could climb up into it and from there you could see almost over the top of the high hedge. However, Sam was not supposed to climb it for fear of falling down and hurting himself.

'Look, Fernando!' Sam cried. 'Watch me!' He made himself wings out of a corrugated cardboard carton and an old feather duster and tied them on at his wrists and shoulders. Zooming over the lawn he climbed up into the tree so rapidly that it did almost look as if he were flying. He stood on the topmost branch sweeping his wings up and down, and his wild free cries had a real echo of distance in them. It was as if all the journeys locked up inside him were crying out aloud against the high hedges and the closed gates. But Fernando Eagle shook his head and looked back over his shoulder longingly to Great Aunt Angela's kitchen.

'Blow!' thought Sam. 'He's not getting the idea. If only I had another tree ... one's not enough for a proper tree-to-tree exercise.' An idea came to him, and he went into Great Aunt

Angela's tiny tool-shed and brought out her all-aluminium-extendable-collapsible   step-ladder and stood it close to the tree. He stuck it all over with pieces of hedge and fallen leaves.

'Look, Fernando!' he said, pointing at the tree. 'Tree! Tree! Get it?' Fernando pretended to scratch his ear with one foot while balancing on the other, and Sam was encouraged by this display of skill. He pointed to the step-ladder. 'Another tree!' he said slowly and clearly, though he had to admit, secretly, that it did not look very like a tree in spite of all his work. 'Another tree! Two trees! Now watch!' Waving his wings gracefully he climbed the step-ladder, stood there beautifully balanced and then leaped from the step-ladder into the top branches of Great Aunt Angela's tree. He did this supremely well . . . he really did look as if he were flying. But unfortunately Great Aunt Angela chose that moment to look through the kitchen window, just checking up.

'Sam!' she screamed. 'Oh Sam! Oh! Come down at once, you inconsiderate boy! What's got 49 into you? Are you trying to drive me to my death?'

'I was teaching Fernando how to fly,' Sam began to explain, but it was no use. He was called untidy, dirty and dangerous, the sort of boy who would set a bad example to a pet.

'Fernando doesn't *need* to fly!' Great Aunt Angela declared. 'He doesn't *want* to fly. Look, you've made him hide his head under his wing, poor thing. And he's been a model bird all day. I was worried to begin with, he was so brightly coloured he looked a bit raffish, but his feathers are beginning to lose that flashy patchiness and settle down to a nice quiet grey.'

And so they were. Parts of him were about the same colour as Sam's school uniform.

'That shows he's happy!' said Great Aunt Angela with satisfaction. 'So don't upset him.'

Sam felt desperate. It seemed to him that if Fernando Eagle couldn't learn to fly, he, Sam, would live for ever behind high hedges and closed gates until all his journeys withered and

died inside him. 'Go here! Go there! Up . . . up
. . . away . . . awa-a-ay . . .' called the voices in his
head and he thought Fernando Eagle must hear
them too. But he didn't. He ate platefuls of bread
and jam and grew neater and more school-
uniformish day by day – taller too. Now he was
just the same size as Sam himself.

Great Aunt Angela knitted him a little blue
scarf and a blue woolly cap with a white tassel,
and fussed over him more and more. It was as if
Fernando was the real person in the house and
Sam just some sort of unnecessary ghost who
had got in behind the high hedge by accident.
One day when Sam and Fernando were on the
lawn doing nothing much, Sam flapping his arms
in a tired fashion and Fernando looking the
other way, Great Aunt Angela came out of the
house in her good going-out coat pushing her
shopping trundler in front of her.

'Norton!' she called. 'Norr-ton! I'm going
down to the supermarket. You may come with
me if you like and push the trundler.'

Sam was astounded to hear Fernando Eagle reply in a very ordinary voice, as if he had been talking ever since he was hatched out of the egg, 'Yes, Aunt Angela! I'd love to. Does Sam have to come as well?'

'Who's Sam?' the Great Aunt said. 'Some little imaginary friend of yours? Now, Norton, don't become too fanciful. Too much fancy is a very dangerous thing for a growing boy.'

'I will be careful, Auntie, I promise,' answered the foolish bird. 'I really will. May I push the trundler all the way to the shops?'

'Of course you may,' replied Great Aunt Angela graciously. 'You deserve a little treat. You've eaten up your greens and your bread and jam so well lately.'

Sam watched them as they set off down the drive. He felt lonely because, though he had never got on very well with Great Aunt Angela, she was the only relation he had. But more than that, he felt desperate for Fernando Eagle.

'One last chance!' he thought. 'One last

chance for him to see that he doesn't have to stay here. He can fly away and be free.'

'Fernando!' he called. 'It's your last chance. You must fly. You must FLY.' He ran down the drive after them and all his imprisoned journeys rose up inside him like leaping flames. 'Like *this*, Fernando!' He held out his arms and the world turned under him. Aunt Angela carefully closed her gate but Sam went up over it and did not come down again. The air took him into itself. He, Sam, was the one to fly.

As if he had been flying for years he rose up higher than the high hedge and saw the whole street beyond – the traffic-lights winking at him and the shops behind the traffic-lights. He even thought he could see the pet shop man at the pet shop door.

'Up and away!' said a voice like a bell ringing in his head. He had often heard it before but never so clearly and now he could do what it told him to do. Up and away he went, between the painted roofs and the chimneys, frightening 53 sparrows, scolded by startled starlings. Up and away, over the chimneys now, and suddenly all directions were possible for him.

The city looked at first like a game of noughts-and-crosses being played beneath him, and then like a great clockwork Christmas present, muttering to itself while lights flashed on and off.

'Up and away!' said the voice like a bell, and a new silvery voice whispered,

'The sea! The sea!'

'Are you surprised?' asked a third voice, but not in his head. This one came from beside him, and there was the pet shop man flying too. 'I saw your Aunt and Norton trembling together by the traffic-lights so I thought you must be up here somewhere.'

Sam thought of Norton and felt sad for the stay-at-home bird. 'I wanted him to be Fernando Eagle,' he said.

'Fernando Eagle never existed,' replied the pet
shop man.

'Believe me, you were the eagle of your Great Aunt's house. There was no eagle space left for a bird to fit into. But there was a Norton space . . . a grey bread-and-jam-trundler-pushing space . . . and he fitted in there exactly. He'll be very happy and so will your Great Aunt. Look! There they go.'

Far below like grey ants, Great Aunt Angela and Norton crawled back towards the front gate and locked it behind them, shutting out the dangerous clockwork city.

'The sea! The sea!' insisted the silver voice and Sam saw that he was indeed set free. Below him lay the world threaded with the bright tracks of a thousand possible journeys. The west wind came alongside him as he flew. A salt taste came into the air.

'You choose!' said the pet shop man. 'It's your first journey. I'll come as far as the beach with you to see you on your way. You'll meet other travellers, of course, but even when you don't you'll never be lonely, for a journey is all the companion a true traveller needs.'

So Sam flew off on the first of his great journeys. He was a boy with somewhere to go and able, at last, to go there, and as he flew the sun shone down on him and turned him from a boy in grey into a traveller of gold.